The Alien's Christmas Baby

C.V. Walter

How to Connect

Follow me on Facebook!

https://www.facebook.com/CVWalter/

Find me online at CVWalterAuthor.com

Read my newsletter and sign up to get it delivered directly to your inbox at https://cvwalter.substack.com/

Contents

Series Information

Molly

Molly rubbed at the muscle on her right side, the one just far enough back to be awkward to rub, and sighed. She was tired, sore, puffy, and starving. The thought of eating, however, still made her want to barf.

She hadn't had morning sickness in weeks but the nausea had left its mark in her recent memory. That someone had definite opinions about what she ate and managed to kick her in the stomach every time she didn't like what her mother ate did not help.

Her comm buzzed on her arm and she rolled her eyes. The only thing worse than being uncomfortable all the time was somebody noticing that she was uncomfortable all the time. There were reasons to monitor her pregnancy closely but she almost wished for a less attentive husband.

Almost.

"Are you well, *cherna*?" he asked when she raised her comm to look at it.

"I'm fine," she said. "How the heck do you know I'm uncomfortable before I do?"

He flashed her a grin that told her he was going to be irritating. "I don't, I have just made a note of what certain measurements mean. Are you uncomfortable?"

She gave an irritated sigh. "I'm fat, slow and starving," she said. "Of course I'm uncomfortable."

"Have you eaten anything besides the crackers for breakfast?"

"No," she admitted. "And I don't really want to, either. I'm craving something but there's nothing that I'm really willing to risk tasting twice."

"You haven't been physically sick in almost six weeks," Mintonar said. "You should have a snack. Would you like me to come feed you?"

The warm tone in his voice when he made the suggestion brought color to her cheeks. "You're busy," she said. "I can feed myself."

"You can," he agreed. "And yet you haven't. I am happy to take the time to feed you if that is what you require."

She sighed. "No, I appreciate it, but no. I'm a grown adult. I'll do what any grown adult would do."

"I'll warn the cook that you'll be coming by the kitchen, then," he said. "Are you craving anything in particular?"

"Cucumbers," she said. "sliced in a red wine vinaigrette. And buttered toast. And bacon."

Mintonar chuckled. "I will let him know that you will be raiding the cold storage, then."

"I'm going to be horribly rude just going through and taking things, aren't I?" Molly asked. "I don't mean to be, you know."

"Molly, if you knew what you wanted to keep in the storage in our quarters, you wouldn't have to," Mintonar said. "As your cravings have changed day to day, it did not make sense to remove things from the general supplies that would make you retch the next day. There is nothing wrong with putting the food you are likely to eat where you are most likely to go look for it."

"That should be in the fridge in our apartment," Molly told him.

"But it is not," he told her.

They'd been having the same argument for months and she still felt silly going and raiding what was, essentially, an industrial size kitchen for her snacks.

"I have to get over this," she said. "There's no reason for me to have issues smelling things in our fridge."

"I will warn him that you are coming and desire bacon," Mintonar told her. "There will be ample supplies when you arrive."

"He doesn't have to," Molly protested but Mintonar had already cut off the call. He'd gotten better at arguing with her, she had to admit. And she did need to walk a bit to work out the cramp in her side. With a heave and a grunt, she stood up out of the large, comfortable chair that had become her chosen place to sit when she was working.

When she'd first started settling in to a routine, she'd tried working at the table. It was large, convenient and intended for the kind of work she was doing. It was also, she'd soon discovered, an easy distraction. With the connection to the Earth network set up, she could poke around on the different websites she used to frequent, though she'd been warned against posting much.

Hours later, she would stand up to make dinner only to find that she'd stayed in the same position for too long and her joints ached. The bio-nanos would make short work of the damage but the pain still lingered. The big, comfortable chair, on the other hand, put less strain on her joints and encouraged her to only use what she could hold in one hand. If she fell asleep, it adjusted to make her more comfortable, and she didn't get out of it feeling like she'd been beaten with a plastic bat.

At the beginning of her pregnancy, she'd been able to curl up in the chair, tucking her feet against the side while she laid her head against the back and reading. Now, she could reach all the way to the floor and it leaned back when she wanted it to. It was like the best parts of a recliner and bean bag chair if it had electronic controls to move the stuffing. Napping in it had become one of her favorite parts of the day.

Once on her feet, she stretched and felt another twinge in her side. This one made her draw in her breath it was so sharp and she knew she needed to walk for a bit. There would be enough time to get to the kitchen for her to work out the cramp in her muscles.

The smell of the bacon in the kitchen made her mouth water and she discovered she wasn't the only woman in the kitchen getting ready to raid the cold storage.

"Hey, mama," Mindy said, turning to give her a hug. "How you feeling?"

"A little stiff," Molly told her. "And like I'm about ready to pop. I thought I might waddle on down to the kitchen for a snack."

The cook, who had been introduced to her with a name she still had trouble pronouncing, appeared at her elbow with a plate of bacon. Mindy reached for a piece and got a spatula to the back of her fingers for her trouble.

"For the mama," he told her with a frown. "You get some next."

"Look, Broccoli," Mindy told him. "Just because you control the food doesn't mean you can-"

"Broccoli?" he asked, interrupting her. "I am not green! I do not go in soup! For that, no bacon!"

Molly laughed at Mindy's outraged expression as the cook huffed off.

"Rude!" Mindy declared. "Fine, I'll make my own bacon!"

After she took one strip off the plate, Molly offered it to Mindy. "You can have one, if you want. I was going to see if there were any of the cucumbers left."

"Did you put them in your fridge?" Mindy asked, taking the proffered bacon. "I don't think anybody's brave enough to try and take stuff out of your fridge. They should still be there."

The cold storage off the kitchen was more of a refrigerated warehouse than an actual fridge. There were smaller cubes with doors into the kitchen where the cook stored smaller items that were likely to be used quickly and he'd designated one specifically for Molly. Things she was likely to crave or need were placed in the fridge, or in a cabinet nearby that had what looked suspiciously like a sticky note on it with Molly's name. Different types of food had shown up that were high in things Molly was lacking during the pregnancy. Some of them were human foods, like pickles and chips, but others were dishes she'd never seen before with instructions of how to eat them on a sticky note on the top.

"I didn't," Molly said. "I wasn't really feeling them until today but there were some brought up with the last round of wedding supplies."

"For the traditional cucumber sandwiches," Mindy said with a nod. "At the, what, traditional Friday Wedding Tea?"

"Bridal shower," Molly said. "And don't laugh, it's actually a thing. We had them at mine and, I swear, they were the only thing worth eating."

"You were pregnant for that one, too, weren't you?" Mindy asked.

"Yep," Molly nodded and opened one of the small refrigerators. Nothing looked particularly cucumber like so she shut it again and reached for the one below it. As soon as she started to bend, the muscle in her back twinged again and she frowned.

"I'll check," Mindy said and squatted down to look through the lower coolers. "You stand up straight and stretch a bit, mama."

"Why are you going through my coolers?" the cook demanded, coming back around the corner with a plate of bacon. "I even made a cooler that was easy for you to get to. Get out. What do you want?"

"Cucumber?" Molly asked plaintively. "With the red wine salad dressing?"

The cook sighed in frustration and shoved the plate of bacon at Molly who squealed happily at it before going over to her cooler and pulling out a container. He took the lid off and showed it to her. The cucumbers had been marinating in the salad dressing for at least a full day and the smell made her stomach rumble.

Mindy popped up and took the container from him. "Thanks!" she said brightly.

"How did you know?" Molly asked. "I haven't ever ordered this before."

He shrugged. "Dorcas saw you looking at them and gave me a recipe she thought you would enjoy. You will try it and let me know, yes? I did not put in onions because you said they have been giving you heart burn."

"Oh, thank you," Molly said. "I didn't think but yes, that would be traditional in this. Has Dorcas been by today? I'll have to be sure to tell her thank you."

"She is hiding," he said, waving vaguely towards the machine shop Dorcas had been using. Several of the younger crew members had taken to following her around so she'd put them to use building some of the designs she'd brought with her. Some of them had been disappointed and wandered off while others had decided that, even if she wasn't going to attempt to find a mate on the ship, she was worthy of their adoration.

"I'll invite her over for dinner at some point, then, and thank her for helping out," Molly said. "Because I know she gave you about half those recipes."

He shrugged again. "She has been very helpful here. Of course we would make foods that you need first. We must feed the next generation."

Molly smiled at him and nodded. "And the next generation is insisting on food before she starts kicking me again. Thank you, Brock."

"Brock," he sniffed. "It's barely better than Broccoli but I will allow you to make your escape this time. Soon, you will be forced to say my name correctly if you want dinner."

Mindy giggled and stepped around Molly. "Thank you, Mr. With Cheese."

He hissed at them and they scooted out of the kitchen like disruptive children. Well, Mindy scooted, Molly waddled quickly, the uncomfortable pressure on her bladder reminding her she was going to need to pee soon and should hurry and eat before it became an issue.

They made it out to the tables before sitting down and setting to their snacks with relish. The bacon was exactly what Molly had been craving and the company was pleasant. Now, if the muscle in her back would stop cramping on her, she'd be a lot happier.

Molly

"What have you been working on?" Mindy asked around a bite of bacon.

"Space law," Molly said before biting into the first slice of cucumber. It was crispy and just sweet enough to not be exactly a pickle. "You?"

"Comparing the nutritional value of the food we brought with us against what the Orvax tend to need," Mindy said. "Not really what I trained in but it's interesting."

"I didn't exactly train in Space law, either," Molly said with a grimace. "I mean, I paid more attention to that than most of the rest but I thought I'd walked away from all that when I quit the practice."

"It never lets you go entirely," Mindy said. "How are you feeling today?"

Molly sighed. "Fat, tired, anxious, ready to be done, and completely unprepared to actually be a mother. Realized just how little I knew about kids and couldn't remember if I knew how to change a diaper. Then didn't know if the Orvax even had diapers or if they used something else and what would they use if they didn't and did anybody bring any with them?"

"So, same as yesterday?" Mindy asked.

"Pretty much," Molly acknowledged.

"What did you find out about the diaper situation?"

"Soft cloth with a water proof outside, can be cleaned in the washers in the various apartments, and they have so many of them I could probably go a month without needing to wash anything but I'm not about to let them stack up in the room."

"Oh, well, that makes sense," Mindy said. "I mean, I guess if they were hoping for kids after leaving the planet. I'm assuming there are a bunch of baby clothes?"

Molly nodded. "Most of them are probably going to be way too big unless she gets a lot bigger before she comes out. I need to talk to Trina about it but I haven't wanted to bother her."

"It's getting pretty close to go time, isn't it?" Mindy asked. "You might want to bug her about it sooner rather than later. She was really looking forward to making baby clothes and I think she could use a break from wedding prep."

"Alright," Molly said with a sigh. "I wanted to take a break from the books for a while anyway."

The muscle in her back cramped again and she reached back to massage it gently. She took another bite of her cucumber and frowned. Walking and eating usually helped with the cramping. Some water was definitely called for, she decided, and maybe a massage from her loving husband if it didn't let up soon.

They finished eating and Molly pulled a water canister from her fridge before they left to see Trina. Water was a vital part of their supplies but they had less issue with it than she would have expected. One of the standard parts of outfitting a ship like this was breaking off a piece of a comet. There were several that orbited Orvax, pulled into orbit over the centuries just for things like this, and they were essentially large chunks of ice and metal. The ships pulled them behind with automated machines going back and forth to break off chunks of the ice as necessary.

As they got closer to the metal at the core of the comet, there was more processing necessary, and the metal was added to the supplies in the machine shop. It made for a nice supply of clean, fresh water and metal to repair parts of the ship. It would also allow them to make supplies for the new settlement whenever they found a place to put it.

It also meant Dorcas had been having fits of delight over the contents of the machine shop.

They wandered over to Trina's studio, Mindy moderating her pace to keep stride with Molly, and got to the door just as Brinker was closing the door behind him.

"Hey, Brinker," Molly called out. "Is she busy?"

He shook his head then looked over his shoulder at the door. "Not as such but I'd give her a few minutes."

"Why, what's up?" Mindy asked. "Everything okay?"

Brinker's usually placid face contorted. "She has a visitor."

"Really?" Molly asked, her face lighting up with delight. "Who? I thought she wasn't interested!"

"If you thought that," Brinker said sourly. "You haven't been paying attention. Give them a few minutes and she'll remember she's mad at him and throw him out."

"You seem awfully sure of that," Mindy said.

"I have been attempting to deliver lunch at various times of the day to avoid walking in on one of their arguments," Brinker told them. "I almost managed but the Captain followed me in."

"Seriously?" Molly asked. "They do this every day?"

"What kind of arguments?" Mindy asked. "Are they sniping at each other? Throwing things?"

"I don't even hear raised voices," Molly said.

"You won't," Brinker said. "But they're fighting. I've walked in on it more than once."

"Are you sure?" Molly asked. "I mean, I know sometimes her tone of voice is-"

The door opened and an irritated Trina shouted. "And don't come back when I'm busy! You can make a damned appointment like everybody else!"

Molly looked at Mindy quickly and Mindy nodded. They waited for the captain to step through the door and grinned at him.

"Good lunch, Captain Cretus?" Mindy asked.

"Good afternoon, ladies," the captain said, nodding to both of them. "I believe you're expected."

He held the door open and they waved at Brinker before heading inside. There were two untouched meals on the café table in the corner and Trina looked thunderous.

"Are you busy?" Mindy asked.

"Always," Trina said with a sigh. "But never too busy for you two. What's up? Come by for lunch?"

"We just ate," Molly said. "But I'd been thinking of stopping by to ask about baby clothes. Mindy said you'd been talking about them?"

"Oh, of course, I was going through the stocks to see what there was," Trina said, walking quickly over to the shelves she'd had set up. "Some of the people here brought generations worth of clothes, you know? The last of their line and all that and it was all handed down and some of it was in such questionable taste, even for an alien planet."

"Polyester?" Mindy asked.

Trina leaned back to look at them. "Worse," she said cryptically and shuddered. She came back out with a basket full of cloth.

"Oh, those are colorful," Molly exclaimed, reaching for the first piece. It was the onesie shape she was used to but there weren't any snaps or buttons that she could see. "How do you get them open to change the diaper?"

Trina ran a quick finger under one of the seams and the fabric parted to the delighted gasps of the women watching. "That's pretty neat," Mindy said. "Do they do that for adult clothes?"

"The overalls in the various shops have something similar," Trina said. "And some of their lounge wear."

"Lounge wear?" Molly asked with a raised eyebrow. "Like casual stuff you wear on the couch?"

"Like lizard," Trina said. "I told you, questionable taste. Someone on board had an ancestor that could give a disco man whore a run for his money in the 'why would anybody wear that' stakes."

"Maybe it was the look at the time," Mindy suggested. "We've had weirder trends on Earth."

"Trust me, easy access pants like this were never a trend in the larger population," Trina said and Molly giggled. "Though I have altered some to do something similar. I never asked why and didn't judge but, trust me, disco man whore is a very apt description."

"I believe you," Molly said. "Do these wear out? Are they going to randomly open and let the diaper fall off?"

"Not so far as I can tell," Trina said. "The way the fabric works is pretty nifty and we've got some stuff that's heading that way in the textiles industry on Earth but I get the feeling this is old tech for them and they've figured out how to keep it from wearing out."

"How did you get them in so many colors?" Mindy asked, flipping through the pile in the basket. "There isn't any white."

"No, the most common color I'm seeing in these is a dark gray, actually," Trina told her. "Which makes sense if you think about it. The bleach we use for disinfecting clothes strips dyes which is why a lot of baby stuff is white. You can boil it and bleach it to get rid of any germs or stains. That would damage their washers but they use this charcoal-y gray soap that strips off all the germs and stuff but tends to leave a little bit of itself behind so it ends up gray."

"Is it actually charcoal?" Mindy asked.

Trina shook her head. "Nah, something else, though the way it's made sounds like someone decided to pee in a campfire and get the best of both worlds."

Mindy laughed and Molly joined her in happily pawing through the baby clothes. "There's other things, too, right?" she asked. "I'm not expected to leave the baby home in these and some blankets until she's old enough to walk, right?"

"Right, like anybody would let you do that," Trina said with a snort. "Of course there's more clothes. I've got leggings and pants for everyday stuff and dresses for the events."

"She's not going to need..." Molly started then caught the look on Trina's face. "At least, I hope she won't need it soon but you're right. Thank you, Trina, I really appreciate it."

Trina sniffed and massaged her hands vaguely while they looked through the basket. "Never know what you're going to be dragged to at this point," she said. "And everyone is going to want to see the baby."

"I hate that she's going to be a part of some of the treaty negotiations," Molly said. "But a healthy hybrid baby is going to be important to show people we can intermarry without problems."

"Are you ready for the comments?" Mindy asked, studiously looking down at the little pajamas she'd pulled out.

"Is it possible to be?" Molly asked. "I'm prepared for the fact that people are going to be hateful. Mintonar has arranged for someone else to take calls from my family and he'll only pass on things he thinks won't hurt me. We've both agreed to keep Aidan out of it as much as we can."

"You've already blocked mentions of you in the news, right?" Mindy asked.

Molly nodded. "I feel like a coward but it wasn't doing me or the baby any good to read some of the first stories."

The muscle in her back pulled again and she frowned.

"Are you alright?" Trina asked. "Do you want to sit down for a minute?"

"I think I should," she said and accepted the chair Trina pulled out from her sewing desk. The chair was comfortable but she couldn't quite get where she needed to be to take the pressure off the muscle in her back.

Mindy looked down at her com and raised an eyebrow. "Molly, you should probably have some more of your water. Sip it slowly but I think it's a good idea."

"Right," Molly said and reached for the bottle. Mindy moved it closer to her hand and pulled another chair over to sit down. "So, do you all have your Christmas shopping done?"

Trina laughed and shook her head. "How do you plan to shop from up here?"

"We still have the internet," Mindy said. "I can have things shipped."

"So you didn't send anything down on the last supply shuttle?" Trina asked.

"Nope," Mindy said. "Well, maybe a couple things. Mostly I sent letters to the people I haven't talked to in a while and pictures of some of what we're doing up here. Had the pictures approved by the Captain, of course, so I wasn't sending anything sensitive."

"So that's why you wanted pictures of us together," Molly said. "I'd wondered."

"No, I just wanted pictures with you ladies," Mindy said. "For me. Because why wouldn't I want to remember this?"

"It is the start of a great adventure," Trina agreed.

"Memaw has been asking after Molly's pregnancy, though," Mindy said. "And wondered how things were going. I told her that, so far, it's been a textbook human pregnancy. Some concerns about how the technology will affect the sprout but otherwise, Molly's been fine."

"And I have," Molly said. "Except for the last week when I just haven't been able to get comfortable but from what I remember, that's pretty normal, too, this close to the end."

"It is," Trina said. "Though there's things we can do if you need us to."

Molly shook her head. "No, walking helps with the worst of it. The belly band Mintonar gave me helps support the bulk so it's pulling less. She's dropped and in place which means weight on just that one spot that aches first thing in the morning and I have to pee every five minutes."

Trina patted her arm and smiled. "You'll be done with this part soon enough and have a lovely daughter to show for it."

"Who will be spoiled beyond belief," Molly said with a laugh then a grimace. "I think I need to get up and walk again."

Molly

Trina helped her out of the chair and Mindy grabbed her water bottle, handing it to her as she started walking around the room.

"Maybe we should start wandering over to Medical," Mindy suggested. "If nothing else, Mintonar can rub that spot on your back that's bothering you."

"Yeah, he's been asking me to come by today anyway," Molly said. "We might as well."

"I need to ask him a few things so I'll come along with you," Trina said.

"Oh, I thought you might have a fitting this afternoon," Molly said.

"I do but not until later. I can take a walk over to make sure you're okay and ask some of the questions I'd been meaning to."

Mindy nodded and they started for medical. "Oh, did you skip your lunch?" she asked, catching sight of the food in the corner.

Trina glanced at it and shook her head. "I'll call Brinker to come and put it away. I wasn't actually hungry when he brought it and I'll manage something later."

"Does he bring you lunch every day?" Mindy asked. "I thought he worked for the Prince?"

"That man is horribly bored," Trina said. "And interfering in my life because of it. I appreciate the care he takes but I suspect it's because he found someone who's less willing to take care of themselves than his actual employer."

"And Kaelin keeps kicking him out when he tries to dress her," Molly said with a snicker. "And it's not even like they have competing tastes, she just likes picking out her own clothes now that she can see the details."

"I'm sure there's more to it than that," Mindy said.

"Yeah, like working really hard at making the second human hybrid baby."

"Third," Mindy said. "And I think they're going to hold off until after the official wedding ceremony. At least, we were talking about if it was possible to time the pregnancy for after the wedding without actually damaging her fertility."

"Wait, back up," Molly said. "You said third."

"Yes, I did," Mindy said. "Anyway, there's just not enough data to know what delaying pregnancy would do and it's such a delicate balance to even make hybrid babies."

"When was there a second?" Molly demanded. "Were you even going to say anything?"

"I was going to wait until after you'd had your baby," Mindy said. "So there wasn't a chance people would divide their attention. You're the one we need to focus on right now."

Trina pulled Mindy into a hug and Molly joined them, bursting into tears as she wrapped her arms around her friends.

"Sorry," Molly sniffled. "I didn't mean to get emotional but I'm just so happy for you! When did this happen? How?"

Mindy giggled and Trina tapped her shoulder. "Pretty sure you know how, Moll," she said. "Same way it usually happens."

"Memaw will claim it was the quilt that did the trick," Mindy said. "She sent it up when I wasn't looking and Alvola made sure to put it on the bed. Pretty sure it happened when we were on the planet, though, so she might even be right."

"Is that the pattern you showed me when you got back?" Trina asked. "Because that is an interesting take on an old variation. How old is the quilt top?"

"Fifty years, I think," Mindy said. "I just know there's a bunch of blankets and throw pillows with the same pattern all over the property and in the town. Pretty sure Memaw's grandmother was giving them as gifts last century."

"That would make sense," Trina said with a nod. "So, when are you planning to tell everybody else your happy news?"

They started walking again and Mindy grinned. "I think Alvola knows. He's made a point of counting when he knows I'm looking but I haven't said anything. Mintonar knows, of course, but right now he's just gathering data. It's too early to do anything but worry that I won't be able to carry to term."

"Oh, that's, yeah, that would be hard. Okay, fingers crossed everything stays healthy," Molly said, crossing her fingers in front of her. "Is there anything you can do at this point?"

Mindy shook her head. "Is there ever? I'm making sure I have plenty of vitamins and continuing to study the needs of Orvax gestation. Which won't be a true crossover because, well, hybrid. Human babies have slightly different needs."

"And we've studied a lot of it but not with the depth possible with the Orvax technology," Molly said with a nod. "Alright, I promise not to hover but please keep me informed with how things go? We didn't catch mine early enough to actually track some of the initial signs."

Mindy gave her a one armed hug and squeezed. "I will. And don't worry, I have the feeling we'll have several opportunities over the next couple years to study a lot of this."

Trina smiled at both of them. "At least I don't have to worry about it," she said. "I can't say I'm upset to be past all the discomfort and sleepless nights you two are going to have in your future."

"I thought Grandma Trina was going to baby sit," Molly said with a wink.

"For a couple hours at a time," Trina said. "Not over night."

Mindy giggled again. "Don't worry, Trina, we know you're going to have your own hands full over night soon, anyway. You might not be having babies but you're going to want to practice making them."

Trina sighed heavily. "Current offers to practice not withstanding, I could really do with the exercise."

"Are you and the Captain still not, you know," Molly asked. "I thought he was interested."

"In far more than I am," she said. "And I need to focus on getting everything ready for the wedding and keeping in touch with my own grand kids. Having the probe up and running has been a real blessing for that."

"How old is your youngest grand daughter?" Mindy asked. "Has she turned two yet?"

"Not until after the first of the year," Trina said. "And I made sure to send down Christmas presents with the last shuttle. I found patterns for an Orvax baby doll poking around through their stuff and I knew Avery would want one."

"That's adorable," Molly said. "I'm surprised you had time to make one."

"They're not complicated," Trina said. "Especially once I figured out how their sewing systems work. I still need to do the fine details by hand but in previous years, I would have needed an entire shop behind me to get everything done. It's gratifying to watch things come together so quickly."

"I bet," Molly said and winced. The cramp in her back and moved to her side and she was feeling a lot of pressure to pee again.

Mindy glanced up at her and tightened her arm around her waist. "You good, Moll?"

"Fine," Molly said, her voice strangely breathy.

"Medical," Trina said.

"Yep," Mindy agreed. They both put an arm around Molly and started taking longer strides.

"I'm fine," Molly protested. "Really, I'm just a little uncomfortable."

"I know you are dear," Trina said. "But you probably want your husband to rub that spot for you, right? And he's in Medical."

Molly sighed. "Alright, we were going that way anyway, you don't have to carry me."

"We're not carrying you," Mindy said.

"We're supporting you," Trina added. "Because that's what friends do."

"I don't, oh," Molly said, letting the pain out with her breath. "That was unpleasant. I think I need my husband."

Mindy looked down at her com and nodded. "Yep, I think you do. How long have you been cramping?"

"A couple weeks?" Molly said. "But I could usually make it go away if I got up and walked around a bit."

"In that one spot?" Mindy pursued.

"Uh, no, that spot started yesterday," Molly told her.

"Well, good to know," Mindy said. "Explains some of the questions I've gotten from Mintonar. You ready to have a baby?"

"I'm not due for another week," Molly gasped.

"Yeah, since when do kids operate on anybody's schedule," Trina said. "And the Orvax gestate slightly differently, right?"

"Shorter," Molly said, clenching her teeth until the cramp eased up.

"So you were due when the baby felt like getting here," Trina told her. "Anything else was a best educated guess based on very little actual information."

"And there's no way of knowing if you're early or late or just on time without more data," Mindy said. "So, off we go to get data."

It wasn't a long walk to Medical but it felt like it took hours. Now that she knew what was happening, Molly was acutely aware of every place her body hurt, every twinge of pain in places that should have been unrelated.

The door to the Medical Bay opened and a warm gush of liquid ran down her leg the minute she stepped in.

"Well, that's indicative," Mindy said, not bothering to look down. "Mintonar!"

Molly looked up to see her husband coming for her with a happy and concerned look on his face. "Is everything all right?"

"Baby's on the way," Mindy said. "Water just broke, you've got about ten minutes between contractions but they're coming faster and stronger so you're going to want to see how much room she's got and how far she's got to go."

He blinked at her. "Oh, I wasn't expecting it this soon."

"I don't think anybody was, Doc," Trina said. "And she's fine for now, it's just been a while since she's had a baby. I think most women with that much time in between tend to forget some things."

More pain shot through her as another contraction hit. She breathed and squeezed the hands Mindy and Trina were holding out for her until it passed.

"Less time now," Mindy said. "Do you want her on a table or a chair? She's going to need to walk around for a bit, I think, to help with the restlessness."

"Chair," Mintonar said decisively. "But, and excuse me for my ignorance, why is she in pain?"

All three women looked at him then Molly started laughing. "Your people don't do labor pains, do they?"

"Pressure, certainly, and carefully calibrated indications of when the baby has shifted and the body is ready to let them out," he said. "But certainly no pain."

Mindy and Trina helped Molly to the exam chair he'd indicated while he pulled out the equipment she was going to need. There was a lot of equipment. "Was that always the case?" Mindy asked. "Like, how long have women been having babies on your world without any pain?"

"For as long as I've been aware of it," he said. "Though it was treated like a recent advance so I'd say some time in the last century or so."

"How long have you had the bio-nanos?" Mindy asked. "About twice that, right? And they were originally intended as emergency things. To stop internal bleeding and repair damage to things that couldn't be repaired with normal surgery, right?"

"Yes," Mintonar said. "And they kept getting better. We use them for most things now. It's what makes this era of exploration possible. Before, there were many dangers trading with other planets."

"I think your scientists short-circuited the pain response in pregnant women," she said.

"We do not want them to suffer needlessly," Mintonar told her. His eyes darted to Molly as she gritted her teeth and grabbed Trina's hand. "I was monitoring her labor with the bio-nanos. It shouldn't have been critical for another few hours."

"Oh, goody," Molly said. "Were you going to tell me you knew I was in labor?"

"I suggested..." Mintonar started then shook his head. "I should have thought. How can I help?"

"She has a cramp right there," Trina said, pointing to Molly's back. "Do you need to be doing anything else right now?"

"No," he said, and rushed to take Trina's spot next to Molly. She grabbed his hand and the look of angry concentration on her face shifted.

"Oh," she said, the relief in her voice palpable. "That's so much better."

Mintonar reached down behind her and started working his fingers over the muscle that had been plaguing her the last couple days and she leaned forward in relief.

"Well, I'm noting that for the log," Mindy said. "You keep doing what you need to, Doc, I got the rest of this."

Mindy

Mindy was making notes during a hard contraction when her com buzzed. Dorcas was looking for her and had questions about something to do with the food. Molly looked to be handling the labor well, especially with Mintonar holding her hand and stroking her skin where everything hurt.

"Hey, Molly," she called, holding up her wrist. "Dorcas is looking for me. Are you good if she stops by or do you want this to be a closed theater?"

Molly laughed. "It's not like I expected any of this to be private," she said. "I'm surprised I can't see the cameras that are recording me for posterity."

"I would not-" Mintonar said and Molly put a hand over his lips.

"Stow it. I knew exactly what was going to happen when I came up pregnant. We have enough unknowns with all of this, I want to make sure we have as much information as possible for the next girls." She took a hard breath and worked to let it out through the next contraction. "I'm okay, I'm not upset, and I appreciate the care you've taken so far."

"So, you're good with a Dorcas visit?"

Molly nodded and Mindy responded with her location.

"Hey, didn't her family raise cows?" Molly asked with a short laugh. "If she sticks around long enough, maybe she'll want to catch."

"Dorcas doesn't really do babies," Trina said. "But I'd be surprised if she wasn't willing to roll up her sleeves and deliver you in the middle of a corn field."

"Rice paddies are easier," Dorcas said, walking through the door. "But we can do this in the middle of a field if you'd prefer. Don't know why, this is nice digs for a delivery room."

"Nothing like my last one," Molly said with a snort that became the breath for another contraction.

"Well, the company's better," Dorcas said. "Do you need a hand in here? I just came to get some information from Mindy but it looks like you all are busy."

"You can keep us company, at least," Mindy said. "I didn't know you'd delivered a baby before."

"Did EMT training before heading out in the field. Seemed like a good idea to have more than one person who knew how to treat an injury if we were going to be away from civilization. My first first field trip as a PHD candidate, one of the girls was pregnant and the baby decided to come early. She'd been cleared to go hiking and we weren't going far but the baby didn't feel like waiting for the helicopter."

Dorcas shook her head. "Babies were never good about keeping to a schedule. Up to that point, my knowledge was largely cows which seem to prefer being born at the most inconvenient times possible, and theory from class."

"Congratulations," Mindy said. "You officially have more practical experience than the rest of us. Feel free to stick around and see the first hybrid baby born on the ship."

Dorcas raised an eyebrow and looked at everybody else. "Really?"

"Really," Trina said with a wry grin. "The Orvax are having what you'd call a fertility crisis. At least some of that is manufactured but I think we have a clue as to some of the rest of it, now."

"What do you mean?" Mintonar asked, then turned his attention back to Molly as she worked her way through another contraction.

"We'll tell you when you're older," Trina told him. "You just focus on getting Molly through this."

Dorcas joined Mindy at the monitors and started asking questions. By the time she understood everything Mindy knew about what was going on, she'd started rolling up her sleeves.

"Medical gloves?" she asked and Mindy pointed to the drawer by the sink. She let Dorcas scrub her hands first before offering to help her put on the gloves. She didn't need to bother, though, because Dorcas had figured out the system Mintonar had set up to allow him to work in the Medical Bay without assistance.

Mindy took her turn and put her own gloves on, working slower with the unfamiliar system than Dorcas had. By the time she was done, the chair had been leaned even further back and

"This thing does predictions," Dorcas said, pointing at the screen with the pertinent measurements.

"Yes it does," Mindy said with a satisfied grin. "I doubt they'll be accurate but, whoa..."

The line showing the intensity of Molly's contractions spiked and the prediction timer jumped from forty-five minutes to ten minutes.

"Guess nothing about this baby is going to be normal, huh?" Dorcas said.

"I think this baby is going to help us define what normal should be," Mindy said. "Or, at least, point at the places where maybe things have gone to far."

Mintonar shifted his wrist to pull up instructions on his com in a way that Mindy still hadn't managed to replicate and a holographic projection of the baby in uteri was in front of them.

"Oh, that's nifty," Dorcas breathed, then stooped down to check on Molly. She was ready to go and they all got to watch the process while Molly pushed her daughter into the world.

The cleanup was quick and mostly painless. After the baby was delivered, the bio-nanos started working on something they seemed to consider an open wound. They were, technically, correct.

There was always more to do after a baby was born than most people realized, and certainly more than the movies and television shows showed, but it went faster with the help from the Medical Bay once Mintonar was able to stop holding Molly.

He left Trina cooing over the squirm bundle on Molly's chest and started setting up the testing they were going to have to do.

"It'd be nice to let her just have some time with the baby," Mindy said softly. "I know this is all important but she could use the pink time."

"Pink time?" Mintonar asked.

"The afterglow," she explained. "When the good pain killers are still working and everything else is soft and has a pink tint to it. She deserves some of that."

Mintonar nodded. "We never got around to starting the good pain killers but I understand."

"What?" Mindy asked. "What do you mean you never started the good pain killers. I thought that's what you were doing?"

"Molly said she didn't want to do anything that might interfere and harm the child. Since this is the first hybrid baby and there's no way of knowing what would harm the child right now, I didn't start any protocols. I'd turned off any processes from the bio-nanos that could possibly interfere already so those wouldn't have done anything, either."

"So what did you do?" Dorcas asked, the look on her face intensely curious.

"I touched her," Mintonar said. "There is the recognition and it gets stronger as we bond more. I suspect it did more to help with Molly's pain than anything I could have done for her otherwise."

"I didn't realize it was so strong," Dorcas said. "What else does it do?"

Mindy opened her mouth then looked up at Mintonar. "Honestly? As far as humans are concerned, we really don't know. A magnificent cocktail of hormones and feel good sparkles but beyond that? We just don't know."

"Hmm," Dorcas said with a nod. "That is interesting. And actually answers some of what I was going to ask about with regards to the food. There's some chains in the vegetables from their home planet that I don't recognize and don't correlate with anything we have. I need to know what they do so I can see if it's something we can cobble together or not."

She looked over at Molly and the baby and gave a small smile. "It can wait, though. I suspect you're going to be busy for a while."

Mindy nodded. "Send them over. I'll get to them faster if I have them already."

"Can do," Dorcas said, and turned away to pull off her gloves and pull her old ones out of her pocket.

A glimpse of pale flesh was all Mindy saw before the gloves went on. Dorcas turned and smiled, giving them a small salute before she left the Medical Bay.

"Does she know she doesn't have to wear gloves on the ship?" Mintonar asked, starting the initial scans on the control panel next to him. They were unobtrusive enough that Molly could hold the baby a little longer without having to move.

"I think she just likes them," Mindy said. "She didn't seem to have a problem with using other gloves and I've never seen her not wearing them."

"I see," Mintonar said. "Well, if she wants other ones, I'm sure we can arrange for them."

"I'll mention it," Mindy said.

They both turned towards Molly and the baby and Mindy watched Mintonar's face soften. Whatever else they had to do, the look on his face was enough to tell her that he was going to make sure he did everything he could to ensure that Molly and the baby were okay.

Kaelin

Kealin was excited. Word had gone out that Molly's baby was on the way and her latest shipment from her mom had arrived just in time.

One of the first things her mom had negotiated for was the ability to send relief supplies to the women on board the ship. The Orvax had agreed and the governments involved had agreed that it would be the humanitarian thing to do. After all, they couldn't leave the women living without basic necessities. That the basic necessities had basically excluded weapons but included little else had left room for all sorts of things to be sent up as humanitarian aid.

Including Christmas decorations.

Once they'd announced their wedding, they started getting things to prepare for the wedding, too. They were trying to publicly thread the Human and Orvax wedding traditions which was going to mean at least a half dozen publicized meals. The wedding planner had been disappointed about not being able to do her job from the ship but she hadn't been given permission to leave the planet.

There were daily, sometimes hourly, calls to arrange things and Kaelin had to handle most of them. If she'd had the time to interview and hire an assistant, she could have handed some of it off to her, but she didn't dare shove as much work as was available on Brinker.

Today, though, was Christmas Eve.

Christmas had always been one of her favorite holidays and she had tried very hard not to be disappointed that there wasn't going to be the usual festivities on board the ship. The Orvax had been very nice and tried to help them adjust to a life that didn't have many outside markers of time or seasons but it still would have felt weird to go caroling through the ship.

When she'd mentioned her disappointment to her mother, she'd encouraged her to make decorations like they used to when she was little. That had almost worked and she had several long strings of paper garland to show for it.

The inclusion of a case of things as "a little something for the holidays" had been unexpected and deeply appreciated. Her happy tears had sent her nearly unflappable *ajoian* into a fit of worry that she'd found adorable. Now, she had taken over part of the lounge to put up decorations.

There was a view screen that could be used for movie nights or presentations that was currently showing the view of the outside of the ship. She'd put garland around it with the help of some removable hangers and was in the process of decorating the tree when Chaegar came in to find her.

"There's a box for Molly," he said. "Your mom sent it but Molly's a little busy. Do you want me to bring it in here? Or should I leave a message for them that it's waiting in the shuttle bay? She said it was important for them to have set up quickly."

"Probably something for the baby, then," Kaelin said. "Why don't you bring it in here and, if it's not critical, I'll put a bow on it and put it under the tree."

Chaegar looked at the tree in suspicion. "I don't think a bow will help it fit under that."

She smiled at him. "It won't be directly under it. Though, I think I might find a way to lift the tree high so we can. It's just where we say we're putting presents. Most of them are small enough to fit under the lower branches but if there's enough of them, they'll spill out and be stacked around. The big ones usually go in the back."

"Alright, I'll bring it in. You can decide where you want it," he said and left.

Kaelin hummed and looked critically at the tree. It was a very nice looking fake one and her mother had sent a box of ornaments in her wedding colors, along with others she thought would be politically appropriate. There had been suggestions of pictures Christmas morning to disseminate. If they could take them Christmas Eve, it would work out nicely and people would have less time to pick at them. They still would but she'd take what victories she could.

Her mother had sent a pile of empty gift boxes that matched the decorations, too, and supplies so they could wrap things. It had almost surprised her that there weren't decorated cookies in the box except that there had been recipes for old fashioned treats using some of things they'd brought up. She'd hand those to Dorcas when she got a minute.

She'd wrapped the last of the lights around the tree and found the batteries for the pack by the time Chaegar returned with the box. He was right, it wasn't going to fit under the tree.

"Oh, that's perfect!" Kaelin said, clapping her hands. "Molly is going to love that and it's such a human thing to give. We'll have to set it up tonight, though, because I know they won't have time to do it themselves until the baby is too big."

"What is it?" Chaegar asked. "It looks like a miniature bed."

"It's a bassinet," she explained. "For while the baby isn't quite big enough for a crib."

Chaegar nodded and pulled out the knife he'd started carrying with him. It had been part of an exchange and explicitly not a gift from David and Jenna. And it hadn't left his side. He cut along the tape like an old pro and, Kaelin thought, he probably was at this point. He'd been helping all of them between trips to the planet on the shuttle and Dorcas had found him to be invaluable.

She pulled the instructions out of the box while he started pulling the pieces out and setting everything out where she could see it.

"You've done this before?" she asked.

He grunted. "Dorcas likes to have everything where she can see it so we can take inventory before we start. It doesn't always come with all the parts and we have to machine the missing ones. Easier to know that if you know what you're looking at."

"That makes sense," Kaelin said. "Oh, and it has the tools and everything we're going to need with the nuts and bolts. I love it when they do that, it makes everything so much easier."

"The decorations look nice," Serogero said from the entrance to the lounge. "But what are you building?"

"A mess," Kaelin said with a laugh. "That will eventually be a bassinet."

"Bassinet?" he asked, tilting his head to the side. "Some form of basket?"

"For the baby," she explained. "Mom sent it up as a present for Molly and I thought it would be nice to have it together for her once the baby got here."

"That is very thoughtful," Serogero said. "I would have thought you'd want to be in the room when the baby was delivered."

Kaelin shook her head and looked down at the instructions. "I like babies but I don't know much about them and I really don't like hospital rooms, even the ones here. Molly doesn't need me as a spectator and I can do this for her."

Serogero kissed the top of her head and she felt a warm glow rush through her that had little to do with recognition. "You are a good friend, my heart," he said. "Is there anything I can do to help?"

"Are you done for the day?" she asked, looking up at him.

"I am and for tomorrow, as well, since we are observing your holiday," he said. "With appropriate documentation and permission for distribution, of course."

Kaelin sighed. "I knew I would be living in a fish bowl," she said. "But at least I have some say about what they get to see. Everything is ready for pictures and I'll make sure we get some with presents stacked under the tree. We'll probably have to stage several and mom sent mistletoe."

"I am at your disposal," he reminded her and laid a gentle kiss on her lips. "And happy to pose for any pictures you'd like to take. This is probably a good time to get some of the others some practice."

She smiled at him. "Agreed. Now, let's build a baby bed that we'll have to hide in half the pictures."

"I thought we were publicizing the baby," Serogero asked, kneeling down to finish unwrapping the pieces.

"We are," Kaelin said. "But babies tend to sleep a lot and are not always photogenic. If we don't want the baby to be front and center in the pictures, we need to hide the bassinet or people will be looking for unflattering angles."

"Are your people that shallow?" Chaegar asked then shook his head. "Never mind, don't answer that. I already know the answer."

"Not everybody," Kaelin said. "Not most of them, really, but these are going to be publicity shots. We're trying to convince people that the Orvax are good and happy people and make good and happy babies, even if we all know that the babies will do what all babies do."

"And what's that?" Serogero asked. "They tend to be a bit rare on my planet."

"Babies poop, pee, sleep, eat, and cry," Kaelin said. "And for a while, that's all they do, though not all at the same time. It is a very rare baby that doesn't do at least some of that in its sleep which makes them all have moments that are not exactly photogenic."

"But they have moments that are perfect for capturing," Serogero said. "And we'll make sure to get those."

"We'll make sure to set up as many as possible," she said. "And I want to do some 'waiting for baby' pictures. So, we'll need to start with that piece there."

She gestured at one of the bars with her foot and Chaegar grabbed it and the next one she indicated. He fitted them together and Serogero had the screw and the tool ready for it. Together, it took them five minutes to get everything but the fabric pieces assembled on the bassinet. Those took another ten when they struggled to get everything in just the right place the first time but it looked just like the picture on the box when they were done.

Chaegar was already gathering all the trash together when Kaelin declared the project a success.

"Alright," Kaelin said. "We'll get all this cleaned up and I'll pretty everything up so we can take a picture and then I'll go check on Molly."

"Do you think something is wrong?" Serogero asked. He was helping pick up the trash and it struck Kaelin as something he didn't usually do.

"No," Kaelin said. "But I haven't heard anything in a while and I didn't think it would hurt to just take a peek and see where everything is at. If something were going horribly wrong, I think we'd be hearing something at this point but I don't want to make assumptions, either."

"I will go with you, then," Serogero said. "And bring the birthing gift."

"You guys do birthing gifts?" Kaelin asked, taken aback. "You didn't say anything."

"Normally, they'd be brought by family and friends," Serogero said. "But it's traditional, if a family is known to the Imperial Family, to wait until the emperor has given his gift to bring yours."

"And gifts are given after the baby is born?" Kaelin asked. "Was there something I could have done to help with it?"

"Usually after a successful live birth," Serogero said. "You have been so busy, I did not want to ask you to do this when I was perfectly capable. I suspect we will have multiple opportunities to shower the mother and baby with presents."

Kaelin smiled up at him. "Actually, I asked mom to send something. We generally do our gift giving before the baby is born but it's been so busy, it was hard to figure out what she actually needed and there wasn't exactly anywhere for her to register."

One of the boxes her mother had sent contained a reindeer with a worried expression and a rattle. There was another one with skin softeners and foot cream she knew Molly would appreciate. Kaelin retrieved the box and joined her *ajoian*.

Dorcas

Dorcas hurried from the Medical Bay, tugging absently at her gloves, and nearly ran into Kaelin and Serogero. She did a double take and blushed, looking vaguely away from Kaelin's face when the other woman laughed and caught her before she could hit the wall when she moved abruptly away from the couple.

"Everything okay?" Kaelin asked, letting her go as soon as she was steady on her feet.

"Fine," Dorcas said, then took a breath. "Better than fine, actually. The baby is here, appears to be healthy, and Molly is smiling and tired. I'm going to go and finish what I was doing before Molly went into labor. If you'll excuse me?"

She dropped a quick curtsy and skirted around them before they could object. Strictly speaking, she didn't have to show any kind of obeisance to Prince Serogero but it felt odd to not at least acknowledge his position on the ship.

If she kept her head down, she'd be able to get through the next few days without any other incidents and then the whole new baby thing should have worn off and she'd be able to stand being around the little critter. It would be crying and covered in snot at some point and she wouldn't want so hard to pick her up and hold her.

Babies took too much time and she'd decided ages ago that she just wasn't interested. Her studies and then running the farm took up too much of her brain power, even if she refused to admit she was keeping up with the latest research and ached to get her hands on more of the random stones on the ship. The ones Trina had kept aside as unsuitable for the jewelry she was putting together to trade had been fascinating and she needed to comb through more of the clothes to see what else was available.

She'd be doing more of that after the holidays. Right now, everything on the ship except for the major functions, had come to a halt for Christmas and the Prince's wedding. They were planning it for Valentine's Day but still hadn't come to an agreement about where it was going to be held. More and more, she was grateful that it wasn't her wedding that was putting her at the center of all of that.

How Kaelin could stand it, especially with all the talk surrounding her face and the fact that she'd stopped wearing glasses, she didn't know. Just the thought of it made her want to take to her bed with a fainting spell.

Or, it would, if she was prone to those kinds of things.

Instead, she went and hid with her machines and her rocks, and continued her research into how food worked for the Orvax. Food was always important when researching a new culture and wars had been fought over water on both their planets, though not as recently for the Orvax. She'd enjoyed getting lectures from Barruch-di-vry, the cook, about the different traditions that went with the meals he prepared and how long he'd had to study to get some of them right.

She'd promised to show him some of her favorites and then work with him to figure out how to adapt them to the Orvax. Not now, though.

Right now, it was Christmas Eve and she was acutely aware of the fact she was very far away from her family. It was her choice, especially since she'd turned down a ride back to the planet to visit, because she wanted to be on the ship. She'd never expected to have the chance to go to space and explore alien worlds, even if it was just through the baubles and stories they brought with them.

There were rumors of people attempting to save the women on the ship for their own good and she wanted nothing to do with that nonsense. Which meant she was going to miss watching her niece and nephew open the books she'd gotten them for Christmas. Objects they loudly protested about for approximately thirty seconds and then curled up with to read while their parents cleaned up the living room. Often with a cup of hot chocolate cooling because it was forgotten about.

She was almost to the lounge, lost in memories of Christmas Past, when she ran into a very solid chest. Strong hands caught her around her upper arms and she relaxed before she could stiffen and step back.

"Careful, Dorcas," Chaegar told her. "I almost knocked you over. You were lucky I wasn't carrying anything heavy with me."

"My apologies, Chaegar," she said, straightening her dress to conceal her fluster. "I didn't think anybody would be through here this late. It is late, isn't it?"

"Yes, ma'am," he said with an attempt at an accent. It wasn't quite as terrible as the last time he'd tried it on her and she smiled.

"Okay, good," she said. "Otherwise my eyes were going as well as my mind. I might still be crazy but I'm at least able to tell what time of day it is."

"You're not crazy, Dorcas," Chaegar told her. "Though you were moving pretty fast to not be watching where you were going. What were you thinking about?"

"Christmas cookies," she told him with a slight smile. "And how I didn't make any this year. Barruch says your people don't really do cookies?"

"Not how we've seen them, no," Chaegar said. "But I think I recognize the word. It's on here, right?"

He held out a packet of papers she hadn't noticed in his hands and she took it from him. It was a stack of recipes with, not just instructions, but explanations about why they worked. Most of it was familiar but some of them broke down the history of some of the grains and what others had branched off and how the texture would differ if they were used in a similar recipe.

"Oh," she breathed, flipping through the pages. "Oh, yes, that's exactly what these are. Where did you find them?"

"Kaelin said they were for you," he explained. "Said they were in a box her mom had sent up to go with the tree. She and Prince Serogero forgot them when they went to go see the baby and I figured I could bring them to you so you'd have them."

"Thank you," she said and looked up at him. "Where were you going that you didn't see me when I bumped into you?"

He grinned at her. "I was trying to read what it said. I think I've had the most exposure to your language in writing besides the Prince. Mostly labels and things but I'm trying to piece it together. It's going to take a bit before we get an actual translation on the writing anywhere close to good."

She smiled. "Still have issues with it on Earth but it's getting better. Do you think Barruch is still in the kitchen to help me figure out how to make these? We've put some of the grains through the mini-mill and I think there's enough to do a batch or two."

"He was there when I left," Chaegar said. "I can come help and between the three of us, we can make the first Orvax-Human cookies."

She laughed. "Much better than babies," she said, brandishing the recipe pages. "These can be eaten."

"Can't really do that with babies," he said with a sad shake of his head. "The parents get mad."

She smacked him with the pages and he laughed. "You don't bake babies," she told him. "You have to roast them with sauce."

He snorted at her taking the joke further and winked. "I don't think we have a pan big enough, anyway. Should probably stick to the cookies."

"If the cookies are sticking, you're using the wrong pan," she winked back at him and they walked companionably towards the kitchen.

Barruch was there, wiping down the counters she liked to use and had the bags of flour she'd brought by earlier. When she walked in, he looked up and smiled at her.

"Ah, he found you faster than I expected. There are new recipes to try!"

She smiled at him and his enthusiasm. "Yes! And we must make them tonight so we can set them out for Santa Claus."

"Who's Santa Claus?" Chaegar asked. "And why does he get cookies?"

The mischievous smile Dorcas could feel on her face made the two Orvax look at each other. "I should probably tell you the actual story before I tell you some of the history behind the belief," she said. "And there's so many songs I can teach you!"

"Do any of them have to do with cookies?" Chaegar asked.

"None of the traditional ones," Dorcas said. "But if we get them done fast enough, I'll see if I can't get a copy of the one song I know about Christmas cookies to play while they're baking."

"Well, if that is not the best excuse I've heard to get to making the cookies quickly, it's the most original," Barruch said.

"Tell me what we need, Dor, and I will get it. You and Barruch can work out the details," Chaegar said, using her pronunciation of the cooks name with a grin.

She giggled and set the recipes out where they could read them. With as much practice as the two had been getting over the last few weeks, they were able to assemble the ingredients and make substitutions quickly. The most basic recipes were variations on things she'd been working out in her head anyway and the only things that really had to be changed were the amounts.

"Dry ingredients, wet ingredients, fat, binder, sweetener," she said, pointing at different things. "You already use the same basic premise in some of your sauces."

"Yes, but what is this recipe? It would not be sweet like your cookies, I don't think," Barruch said. "It would go well with savory foods, would it not?"

"Ah, the base recipe on that is not particularly sweet, though there are sweet corns and some people add sugar or honey to this part to make it sweeter," she said. "My family never did that, though, so it would taste odd to me. We'd add honey butter if we wanted to make it sweet."

"What's it called?" Chaegar said. "Corn something?"

"Cornbread," she said with a smile. "I have very fond memories of my uncle Cole cooking it when it got cold. Usually with chili or a pork roast but sometimes to have so we could make stuffing with it."

"What were you stuffing with it?" Barruch asked. "It's not really substantial enough to hold much of anything up. Not with the ratios in that recipe."

"They used to stuff it in turkeys, along with a half dozen other ingredients, which is a type of poultry. Like chickens but bigger and they taste different. Nowadays, they make it on the side as its own dish but it's still called stuffing."

"Your planet has odd names for things," Chaegar said. "But they eventually make sense, most of the time."

"Not the entire planet, just the language," Dorcas said with a smile. "Although, some of the other languages can get even more convoluted, if you start looking into them."

"We've started adding some of the other languages on your planet to our translators, haven't we?" Barruch asked.

"Damina pushed for a list of the most popular languages in the section of the planet we're dealing with to fix the space station," Chaegar said. "I guess a bunch of people speak different languages."

"Most of the planet has to find ways to communicate with people who speak a different language," Dorcas said. "The easiest way is to learn at least some of the language of the people you're going to be talking to so that makes a lot of sense. Probably makes the translations a bit more difficult to wade through, though."

Chaegar shrugged. "Maybe, but that means I don't have to actually learn them. They're getting mobile translators programmed and setup so it's not just the people who have learned the language that get to go down on the surface."

"Think they'll bring any more people on board?" Barruch asked.

Another shrug from Chaegar. "I don't have any orders keeping people from coming back with me when I get supplies but there are guards to keep humans from getting on the shuttle. I don't think they want to lose more of their people to us than necessary.

Barruch let out a heavy breath. "Figures. Just as I'm starting to figure out what they like to eat, they're not going to send me any more to feed."

Trina

Trina had hugged the new mom, kissed the new baby, then begged exhaustion to head back to her space. She'd forgotten, or possibly never realized, how many emotions a person could feel being in the same room as a woman giving birth.

There had been so many things that could go wrong, so many things that were a surprise, like the way Mintonar touching Molly had eased her pain in ways the best medications on Earth couldn't have. How many more things were they going to learn about the way they interacted with the Orvax?

The whole thing made her tired and she didn't want to think about it anymore.

It was Christmas Eve and she was on the space ship. She wanted to be on the space ship. Not only was she living out a dream she'd never dared think was possible, she was using skills she'd spent a life time mastering to help other people.

Absently, she rubbed at the back of her hands. They ached less with the influence of the bio-nanos but even the best alien technology couldn't reverse the effects of aging and spending all her time manipulating small needles and cranky fabric. It wasn't as bad as it had been when she was on Earth but it was still disappointing that she couldn't get away from the pain even with alien technology.

It might have been the late hour on a holiday but she was feeling every minute of her fifty-five years and it struck her how many of those minutes she'd spent alone. Her daughter had been out and on her own for almost a decade and had spent a lot of the time before that with her father. As good of terms as she'd been on with her ex-husband, a large part of why he'd been her ex had to do with how lonely she'd been living in the same house with him.

Most of the time, she liked her freedom and didn't feel the sting of loneliness quite so acutely as she was that night. The video call with her daughter and granddaughters in the morning would go a long way to make her feel better. She just had to get through the night.

While she'd intended to go to her workshop, she found herself wandering towards the lounge. Kaelin had mentioned setting up a Christmas tree and, while she might personally skip putting up a tree some years, Trina wanted to see the tasteful decorations Kaelin's mother had sent.

The shiny gold and cream ball ornaments didn't surprise her, nor did the teal and gray snowflakes, but she wasn't expecting the reindeer, gingerbread men with horns, and ballerinas with lavender colored hair. Trina was very glad Margaret was on their side and dedicated to making sure her daughter was happy. Her attention to detail was occasionally scary.

The garland over the view screen continued the theme and Trina's eyes caught on the mistletoe that had been hung over the walkway. It was the perfect place for it and an ideal spot for publicity pictures of happy human-Orvax couples. And the odds were good that the Orvax didn't know what it meant beyond it being a part of the decorations.

"Couldn't sleep?" a deep voice said behind her.

She had to keep herself from shivering at the sound and she turned to snap at the man who'd addressed her. The words died on her tongue when she saw him.

Maikedon, Captain Cretus, was not wearing his uniform.

Casual pants that were comfortable but cut to show how fit he still was along with a white shirt that was open at the neck and rolled up his forearms. It was the most relaxed she'd ever seen him. She'd started to suspect he slept in his uniforms.

"Didn't want to go to bed yet," she told him, her mouth suddenly dry. "How did you know I'd be here?"

He shook his head. "I didn't. I stopped by the Medical Bay to drop off my birthing gift and was told you'd just left to go to bed. I'd seen the crate of decorations being unloaded earlier and thought I might come and see what they looked like."

"Ah," Trina said. She turned and looked at the tree and nodded. "Kaelin's mom has good taste and Kaelin did a great job of setting them up. I know a lot of public figures get pictures of setting up their Christmas trees but most of them actually have a professional design and set up everything except the things for the photo op."

"Did anybody take pictures of her setting it up?" he asked, moving to stand beside her.

Trina shrugged. "I don't know. They should have but we were all a little busy."

"She did it all by herself?"

"Yeah," Trina said. "Though I get the feeling there was help with the bassinet. That's the kind of thing that required two hands to get it that neat. And she would want it to be neat for official photos, even if they're not actually publicity photos."

"Surely Brinker could have helped her," Maikedon said.

"He was nagging at me to eat," Trina told him. "You should remember, you were there helping him."

"I did not intend to nag," Maikedon told her after a moment. "You so rarely stop to take care of yourself, I thought you might need the reminder that you, also, are important. Not just the things you make but you, yourself, is important to the ship and the mission."

Trina snorted and he turned towards her.

"Do you truly not believe me?" he asked.

"It's not that I don't believe you," she said, rubbing at her hand. It had started to ache while they stood there and it kept her from having to focus on his question more than it deserved. "I just don't really know how much I actually contribute to the mission beyond making pretty things to trade."

"What's wrong with your hand?" he asked.

"A lifetime of repetitive stress," she said with a wry smile. "It aches when I'm tired."

"You do that often," Captain Cretus said and took hold of her hand. His fingers ran gently over her knuckles and pressed lightly at the places she'd been rubbing a moment earlier.

"I seem to be tired a lot," she said. "Consequence of getting old, I think."

Trina had to fight the trembling that threatened to spread throughout her body. It happened every time he touched her and she wasn't sure how to handle it. Nothing in either of her marriages had equipped her to feel everything he made her feel.

"You are not old," Maikedon said. "You have barely made it to the middle of you life. In fact, I should be ashamed for trying to attract someone so much younger than me. I can't help but hope you'll feel pity for this old fool some day."

"You're not old," she said, determined not to let her voice shake. "You can't possibly be older than me. You've barely got any gray in your hair."

He lifted a hand to her hair and ran a strand through his fingers. "Do you mean this lovely silver is a consequence of age?"

"Yes," she snapped. "And I earned every one of them."

"Is there something else that causes the silver in your hair, then?" he asked, continuing to stroke it while his other hand caressed the back of hers. "Because I refuse to believe it is all due to age."

"Genetics," she said. "And stress."

"Then your family has lovely silver hair and you have endured much," he said. "You told me some of it. Do you regret any of it?"

She sighed. "Not most of it," she said. "I did what had to be done at the time. I wouldn't have chosen most of it but I survived and have the wisdom and gray hairs to show for it."

Every self-preservation instinct told her to snatch her hand back, to pull away from what he represented, but she wanted him. Two previous husbands, both of them in the military, had given her plenty of warning about what being with him was going to be like. And how it was likely to end.

They might be here on a mission of peace but that didn't mean things were going to stay peaceful. She'd lost her first husband to a skirmish during peace time. Her second husband had been broken badly enough inside that he couldn't be there for her as a partner. When they'd divorced, he'd finally realized he needed help and eventually sought it out.

Whatever scars Maikedon had, she wasn't the person to help heal them.

Part of her, though, wanted to see them. Wanted him to see hers. Desperately wanted him to continue touching her hand.

"Your wisdom and your silver hair gives you strength," he said softly. "And a beauty that could not be equaled by a younger woman."

Trina trembled and closed her eyes.

"Thank you," she said. "You don't have to say things like that. I appreciate the sentiment, though, so I won't stop you."

"I am not sentimental," he told her. "Very often, I am a hard man. Hard to serve under, hard to live with, settled in my ways and a creature of habit."

"So am I," she said with a laugh. "You can ask my daughter and my ex-husband."

"I will," he said with a nod. "If only to meet the man who was foolish enough to give you up. And to thank him for making you free to Join with me, should you decide to make me a very lucky Orvax."

A harsh laugh erupted from her before she could stop it and she clenched her teeth to stop the next one. "I still don't know why you insist on that. I'm so far past my fertile window, I think some of those parts have started collecting dust."

"And I have told you, that does not matter to me," he said.

She gave him a wry smile. "It should. Your people need babies and I can't make them."

"My people, yes," he agreed. "But I am too old to raise a little one. I crave something more from my companions than a pretty face and a fertile womb and I am at an age and position where I can cater to my preferences rather than my people's need."

"You can, yes," she said. "But we both know that, if your people asked you to, you'd step forward to do your duty. And I wouldn't hold it against you, even if it broke my heart. Which is why I won't be risking it because I suspect that call will come sooner rather than later."

"Trina," he started.

She pulled her hand gently but firmly from his grasp. "No," she said. "My answer is still the same. I appreciate you and everything you've done. Thank you for letting me stay on the ship. But I can't make the commitment you want from me."

He let her go and she left the lounge, her steps hindered only slightly by her awareness of the mistletoe. She gave it a wide berth and hoped his sharp eyes didn't notice. Something told her he watched ever step she took and would ask someone else about her reasons for doing so.

She wasn't going to think about it for the rest of the night, however, just like she wasn't going to think about the fact that her hands had stopped aching. The rest of her body ached for different reasons but the ache in her hands had stopped almost as soon as the rest of her had started shaking with need.

Mindy

Despite the long night, Mindy was up bright and early to take the call from her family. She'd sent gifts and money to buy something for everyone and had a stack of her own presents to unwrap from them. They'd asked her to wait to open them until they could be on the call with her.

Several sets of slippers and a robe joined the growing wardrobe while her cousins exclaimed over the delicate jewelry or fancy knives she'd sent. It was all lovely and functional but she had the feeling that most of it was going to be put aside for a rainy day since it was all from things on the space ship. All the gifts she'd gotten would be added to the rotation, especially the robe, since they were things she had started feeling in need of.

There were gifts for Alvola, as well, which surprised him. Her family was closed off but had a habit of adopting spouses like they were blood. The box for both of them started the tears running down her face when she opened it.

The quilt they had slept under had been cleaned and folded with care. Between the folds were ancient white linens, worn once per child then carefully pressed and kept for the next generation. They'd been carried on ships before, from one continent to the next, and lovingly preserved.

"Memaw, how could you know?" she asked, holding up the Christening gown and cap. The tiny little socks that went with them were attached carefully with a safety pin, a delicate touch necessary to keep from breaking any of the fibers.

"I didn't," Memaw told her. "But you've been a little weepy lately, Mindy-girl, and I hoped. And I figured if it hadn't happened yet, it would soon, and the quilt couldn't hurt."

"Thank you," Mindy told her. "Really, I don't think we could thank you enough for all this. I don't know that we'll have a christening out here..."

"There will be something," Memaw said. "And we can do the blessing with the video call, if we have to, but you're the next person to need those so you hold on to them until the time's right to pass them on."

"Alright," Mindy said.

"There's another one," Alvola said, holding up a small box. "It's too small to be another blanket, though."

"That one's from me," Jeb said. "You should do it next."

Alvola nodded to the screen and Jeb looked serious. He removed the wrapping from the box and opened it to find four rings inside. Two were simple bands that were anything but plain. They were etched with interconnecting symbols and they matched. The other two also matched but were made of a flexible dark gray material.

"Are those wedding rings?" Mindy asked.

"A titanium set and a rubber set. I know you both work with things that could damage you if it got caught on a wedding ring so those are designed to break and not conduct energy so they can be worn to work."

Mindy smiled and felt another tear gather in the corner of her eye. It had never sat right with Jeb that they didn't wear rings, despite the fact that they were both wearing the signs of his tribe in their skin. And with their child on the way, there wasn't any deeper way to show they were committed for life. Still, it wouldn't hurt to wear the rings.

She offered her hand to Alvola and he pulled out the smaller of the two rings. He took her hand and slipped it on her ring finger, leaning to kiss her as soon as it had slid into place. She repeated the process, complete with kiss, and laughed when her family cheered on the other side of the call.

"You just wanted to see it," she accused.

"Nonsense," Jeb shot back with a grin. "I'd never use my old man's wiles to trick you into letting me see my favorite niece get married."

There was a shout of protest and Jeb laughed. "Alright, my favorite niece who's married to an alien and working on the space ship right now."

Alvola raised an eyebrow at her and she winked at him. She'd noticed the careful way Jeb had hedged his qualification. Bets had been trying to get a ride out to 'help' ever since they'd left but there had been too much security at their other official landings. There were other shuttles in the hold but they were mostly exploratory things, probes with room for one or two operators, and thus weren't suitable for a mission to the planet.

That might not be the case in the future, however, especially if the officials on Earth decided to delay them further than they already had.

"Right now, huh?" she asked.

"Hey, you never know, one of your cousins might take it in their head to hitch a ride the next time someone comes down for wedding supplies. Which I understand isn't until January?"

"Now, now, no talking shop on the holidays," Memaw demanded. "That can wait until tomorrow. Which it almost is here but I know

Mindy's got a full day ahead of her. You'll send us the best pictures that aren't made public, won't you Mindy-girl?"

"Of course," Mindy said. "I was planning on taking some personal ones, anyway. We'll do the family portrait in front of the Christmas tree, too, the way we did when we were little."

"With the folks on the ship, too," Memaw said.

Mindy's grin spread. Her friends had been folded into the family without a second thought. For the moment, all was right with the world. "Alright, Memaw, any requests?"

"You do what you feel's right," Memaw told her. "But give our love to Michael and Chaegar and Damina and tell them I sent stuff up for them, too."

"I'll tell them," Mindy said. "Merry Christmas, I love you."

"Love you, too, Mindy-girl," Jeb said. "Merry Christmas."

A chorus of Merry Christmases rang out from behind him and Mindy laughed before the screen went dark.

"How much of that last shipment was Christmas presents?" she asked Alvola.

He took her face between his hands and kissed her until she was breathless. That didn't take long enough so he kept kissing her until she was leaning against him and trembling with need.

"Merry Christmas, wife," he murmured against her lips. She moaned and wrapped her arms around his neck.

He picked her up and carried her to the bed. Laying her down, he opened the wrap she'd put around her naked body to make the phone call to her family. It wasn't properly a dress and covered less than the robe they'd sent. She'd been flashing long stretches of pale flesh at him during the entire call while her upper half looked demure.

"Merry Christmas, husband," she told him, stretching out to let him get a good look at her body.

He ran his hand over her belly, still in awe of the transformation that would take place over the next year. For now, it was still soft and gently rounded, almost flat, and the muscles clenched where his touch tickled. With a tender kiss, he started his worship of her body at her belly, and started working his way down.

Mindy's hands grasped at his horns when he found the spots she enjoyed being teased. Her grip tightened when he started working his tongue on the center of her pleasure. He added his fingers and pushed her over the edge quickly just to start forcing her pleasure higher.

When they left their room later to join everybody else, they both glowed with satisfaction. Alvola tried not to look smug at how thoroughly he'd pleasured his wife but it was a losing effort.

Kaelin and Serogero were already in the lounge, and had been for a while if the pile of presents and full trays of cookies were any indication. Everything had been arranged and rearranged over and over with Kaelin taking pictures and setting up for the couple to have pictures taken of just the two of them.

Since they hadn't been able to bring an actual photographer to the ship, they'd rigged a camera with a trigger that could be hit with one of Kaelin's fingers or a convenient toe. She was able to see what they looked like in a display off to the side of the actual camera so she didn't have to look far to get the pose right. Accidental triggers were inevitable and some of the pictures of her frustration when they were setting the system up were comical, though Mindy would never tell Kaelin that.

They knew each other through a mutual friend and, as much as Mindy liked Kaelin, they still didn't have the easy camaraderie she shared with some of the other women.

"You look like you've been busy," Mindy said with a nod to the cookies and decorations.

"Oh, the cookies weren't me, thank goodness," Kaelin said with a smile. "Though I've been including them with the pictures. They're just different enough to make the setting feel alien while still being familiar to people as cookies. They're pretty yummy, too."

"Really?" Mindy asked. "Can I have one? Are you done taking pictures?"

"Do you mind if I get a picture of you eating one?" Kaelin asked. "I don't want to force you into our photo shoot but you're dressed for it so it might be okay?"

Mindy smiled at her. "Memaw actually asked for pictures. I was going to ask if you minded taking some pictures for her, too."

"Of course I don't mind!" Kaelin exclaimed. "Honestly, I'm tired of posing for publicity stuff. I'd rather take pictures of all of you enjoying Christmas."

"Well, then, feel free to take a picture of me enjoying this delicious cookie," Mindy said. She held it up long enough for Kaelin to turn the camera on her and then took a bite.

It was unlike any cookie she'd had before; sweet, crumbly, with a vague nutty flavor she couldn't quite place. It was almost, though completely unlike, shortbread. The frosting was colored cream cheese frosting with just a hint of fruit in it.

"Who did these?" Mindy asked. "How did they do the frosting? This is amazing!"

"I don't know," Kaelin admitted. "It goes really well with the cookies, though, right? I need to find out how she did it."

"Who made the cookies?" Mindy asked, grabbing another one.

"I think it was Dorcas," Kaelin said. "Unless Bur-rock did."

"Barruch," Serogero corrected gently.

Kaelin sighed heavily. "I keep pronouncing it wrong. I'll get it right eventually."

"I know you will, my heart," Serogero said with a gentle kiss on her cheek. "I have every faith you will get his name right. So does he."

Mindy hid her smile behind another cookie then stepped away from the plate. They were really good and she was afraid she'd eat the whole batch if she didn't stop.

"Are you eating all my cookies?" Molly asked. Mintonar pushed her gliding chair into the lounge while she held the baby. "I was promised cookies."

"You snooze you lose, Mama," Mindy said. Kaelin laughed and took her the plate.

"Are you okay to be up and out of bed?" she asked while Molly chose a cookie with red and white stripes.

"You'll notice I'm not exactly up," Molly said with a rueful laugh. "But I brought my doctor with me so I have every confidence I'll be well taken care of."

"She could probably walk if she wanted to," Mintonar told her. "However, I would be happier if she rested and let her body heal. Things went better than we could hope but there's no need to tempt fate."

"Learn a new word there?" Mindy asked with a wink. "Your wife is rubbing off on you."

"Yes," Mintonar said with a fond smile. "I could not wish for a better mate."

Damina

"This is a human tradition," Damina protested. "I do not want to intrude."

Captain Michael LaGrange smiled slightly at the alien woman who could nearly look him in the eye. Smart and sassy when she was in her element, she had perked up at the suggestion that she join him for the Christmas party. Now that they were a few steps away from the lounge, she'd dug her heels in and refused to go any farther.

"The other mates will be there," he told her. "It's a family thing. They would never exclude you."

"But we are not family yet," she told him. "And I did not bring anything to give. I didn't know there would be gifts involved."

"I should have told you," he admitted. "But nobody would expect you to bring a gift. In this kind of situation, people unfamiliar with the tradition can't be expected to know to show up with something. Besides, you're going to be offering to baby-sit."

"Baby-sit?" Damina looked horrified. "Why would I offer to sit on a baby?"

"With the baby," he said with a laugh. "You'll sit with the baby so Molly and Mintonar can get some peace and quiet."

"And how will I do that?" she demanded. "I would be happy to, of course, but how would I make such an offer in this kind of setting."

"With this," he said and handed her an envelope with Molly's name on it.

She looked up at him in confusion and he smiled.

"Another Earth tradition. It had different names depending on who is offering it but people who can't give gifts that cost money often give ones that promise time in the future. Inside that envelope is a coupon good for one free evening of baby-sitting. When it's time to open gifts, Molly will open it and be filled with joy that you thought of her."

"But I didn't think of her," Damina said. "Well, no, I always want to be helpful and I can't help but envy what she has with Mintonar but this gift isn't something I came up with."

He took a deep breath. "No, it isn't. I felt bad because I hadn't given you enough warning to get them something. If you don't want to give that as your gift, you don't have to. I should have thought to explain more of what was going to happen today."

She shook her head. "There hasn't been time, really," she said. "You've been so busy with your official duties and the only things I've asked about have been the ones you said I need to know in order to be your mate."

"And you still haven't decided," he said.

"Are you mad?" she asked. "That I need more time?"

"Of course not," he said. "I could never be mad with you about this. You want time to work out what being with me will mean and I want you to be sure, completely sure, that you want to be with me."

"I worry that we do not have the time for me to dawdle," she admitted. "There are so many things I don't know about."

"We will make the time," Michael told her. He lifted a hand to caress the side of her face. "I'll wait for you as long as I have to. And I'll come for you wherever you are. There is nothing that can keep me from you except the command to leave you alone that comes from your lips."

"I can't tell you to leave me alone," she told him with a smile. "I'd miss you too much."

"Then don't," he said. "But do come with me to the Christmas party and give Molly your gift. We will take pictures and show that there is a happy relationship between the Orvax and humanity."

"For now, at least," she said.

"And we'll do our best to keep it that way," he said and kissed her forehead.

The caress of his lips sent a shiver through her that had nothing to do with the temperature on the ship. She'd never had a kiss effect her so much. Part of her was getting used to the casual movement of his hand over her skin and another part of her was hoping it would always give her the thrill she loved so much.

She closed her eyes to savor the feeling for another moment before she took a deep breath and stepped back.

"Better?" he asked and she nodded.

He offered his elbow in the way she'd come to understand was polite for human men in his culture and she tucked her hand inside it. With a surreptitious glance, she admired his uniform and the way it fit him. When he'd told her he would be wearing his nice uniform for the party, she'd pulled out one of the last dresses she'd owned.

It wasn't as formal as some of the ones that had been brought along but it was nice and fit her in ways most of her other clothes didn't. She'd appreciated the warning about what was appropriate and the chance to show it off. He'd done his best to help her navigate the world he was going to be moving in and she knew it was with an eye to a continued partnership.

A few steps took them to the entrance to the lounge where she ended up staring at the decorations, despite the fact that she'd promised herself she wouldn't. She'd never seen anything like it. Stacks of brightly wrapped boxes around a green tree that was so covered in decorations, she could hardly see the branches.

If she hadn't known that trees on Earth did tend to be green, she wouldn't have believed it. Who'd ever heard of green trees? The twinkling lights and shiny hanging balls made it hard to look directly at the tree but the stack of presents took her breath away. She'd never seen so many in one place.

"Damina!" Kaelin called a moment before she had her arms full of her happy friend. "You came! I'm so glad you came. I wasn't sure you would!"

"It was a near thing," Michael told her with a wink that made Damina blush. "But I managed to talk her into it. She even brought a present."

"Really?" Kaelin asked, stepping back. "Oh, and you look so beautiful. Put your present on the pile and come have a cookie. We need to take a picture of you and Captain LaGrange in front of the tree and you can be in the group pictures, too. Do you mind if I take a picture of you eating the cookies?"

"Why do you need a picture of us together?" Damina asked. "Is that traditional?"

"It's..." Kaelin trailed off and looked at Michael who nodded. "Yes, it's traditional. I'm sure you'll want a copy and, even if you don't, I do. So I insist. Now, come have a cookie."

Damina let herself be led to the table with several plates of decorated baked goods.

"These are cookies?" she asked. "What are the designs on them? Do they always have something like this?"

"These are Christmas cookies," Kaelin said with a smile. "The designs are typical Christmas things. That's a snowman, that's a candy cane, a Christmas tree, a gingerbread man, Santa Claus, Mrs. Claus and... I don't recognize that one."

"Ah, that's our Natal Star," Damina said. "A stylized one but it's very distinct."

"What's a Natal Star?" Kaelin asked.

"An old tradition," Damina told her with a sad smile. "In the darkest, longest days of winter, we decorate our houses with them to remind us that spring will come again and the world will be reborn. It's the first star seen on the first night of spring and our long ago ancestors believe it was the cause of the spring re-birth."

"Ah," Kaelin said. "We have something similar. For similar reasons, actually. We can talk about it later, if you'd like."

"I imagine most places that have a winter have something like that. When we were living much closer to death from a failed harvest and the hunger pains from a long winter, it's helpful to know that there will be life again."

Kaelin hugged her and Damina realized she was tearing up. For years, the planet at the end of the star bridges was her Natal Star. The hope for life seemed so far out of reach and suddenly they were here. She'd walked on it, seen the life that thrived on it, and had the opportunity to partake of it.

"Hope is good," Kaelin said. "And where there's life, there's hope. I'm glad you decided to join us for Christmas."

Damina gave the princess a small smile. "For Christmas, yes. The rest, though..."

"The rest will come when it does," Kaelin told her. "Just enjoy yourself today."

"I..." Damina wiped at the corner of her eyes. "Thank you, I will."

"And if you need to talk, I'll make time for you," Kaelin said softly. "I know I seem super busy with the wedding preparations, and I am, but the decision you're contemplating is also important and I might know a bit about what you're looking at."

"I'll ask Brinker to make me an appointment," Damina said and Kaelin made a face.

"I need to hire my own secretary, I think," she said. "So, if you come across anybody you think would like the job, let me know. We're either boring Brinker to death or we're going to work him ragged. There is no in-between, it seems."

Damina nodded. "I will keep it in mind. Do you not think you should bring someone from Earth to help you?"

Kaelin made a face. "I would if they'd let me," she said. "If only to have someone familiar with our customs. Mom's good but she can't be everywhere. Unfortunately, there's been...the suggestion of threats against anybody who would want to help."

"I don't understand why," Damina said. "Isn't it in your people's best interest if the wedding goes well and we become allies?"

"Someone complained about unrestricted travel off the planet," Kaelin said with a sigh. "With the implication that the aliens are going to try and steal all the human women."

"Not all of them, certainly," Damina said. "And, to be fair, we want some of the men, too."

Kaelin giggled and Damina smiled at her. She liked the new princess even if she still wasn't entirely sure how they were supposed to interact. There were protocols, she knew there were, but Kaelin refused to stand on ceremony. If she decided to follow all her instincts and Join with Michael, she'd have to learn all of them so she could be in the public eye without embarrassing the people she loved.

"I don't know if admitting we're taking some of the men, too, would make it better or worse," Kaelin said with a laugh. "We'd probably get a whole lot of volunteers. There's already a petition to let women volunteer to come and mate with the alien men."

Damina gave her a look. "They do realize it's at least partially a matter of chance if they connect at all with any of us, right? I mean, having all of you have the same reactions was a minor miracle. I think a couple of the people we met on the planet were actively repulsed and if that wasn't a weird feeling, I don't know what is."

"No, they don't know," Kaelin said. "And I don't know how much it would help to explain it. There are still going to be people who want to try and become romantically involved with an alien. And others who think they do but wouldn't be able to handle everything else it requires. Recognition isn't exactly a comfortable feeling."

"I think we'll need to explain as we get closer," Damina said. "To keep people from being afraid, at least, and to maybe ease the pain of rejection if they try and it doesn't work out."

"Well," Kaelin said. "It's a good thing we have a nurse as part of the diplomatic crew, isn't it?"

Damina nodded slowly. "Yes, I think I need to make plans about just how much of our biology and technology to talk about."

Molly

Molly had objected to the hover chair at first. She was walking just fine, mostly. A little slowly, perhaps, but she remembered being absolutely wiped out after giving birth to Aidan. Being a little slow seemed like a massive improvement over the last time.

Rather than arguing with her, Mintonar handed her a drink while she was standing. Her hand trembled so badly, she couldn't quite bring it to her mouth. She handed it back and sat down.

"It takes time, *cherna*," he told her. "You are recovering much faster than you would without the help but it is still going to take time."

"I know," she said, and she knew the frustration came through in her voice.

He kissed the top of her head and tilted her face to look up at him. "You will heal. You will do so with a speed that would astound your human doctors. For now, use the tools we have to help you get around easier and let the people who love you take care of you."

She closed her eyes and nodded. "I don't like being weak."

"You're not weak, *cherna*," he said. "You are one of the strongest beings I've ever met. You are healing and that takes time. Now, are you comfortable?"

She shifted in the chair and adjusted her skirts slightly. She was wearing a forest green dress with silver jewelry. Mintonar wore something he'd called a court suit in dark gray with silver details. Trina had brought an infant dress in the same color as Molly's and the softest blanket she'd ever touched in a color that matched Mintonar's suit.

"I'm ready," she told him and he handed her their sleeping infant.

She was perfect. Her skin was a dark blue like her father's, though she'd been told that puberty could change the color dramatically, except the inside's of her arms which were a light cream color. Her horn nubs were little more than a suggestion of a bump, something else that would likely change with puberty.

Her features were tiny and delicate, the perfect mix of human and Orvax, and she could have been a doll rather than a living, breathing baby. All the tests Mintonar had run came back with her being healthy, if slightly small, for an Orvax.

When they entered the lounge, Molly was shocked by the decorations. She'd known Kaelin's mother had sent a few things for Christmas but the amount of boxes around the Christmas tree took her breath away.

The joy she saw on the faces that greeted her warmed her heart and she took a cookie from the plate Kaelin brought her.

"Tell me these are all decoration," she said, her voice pitched low so only Kaelin could hear. "Background for the publicity pictures."

"Nope," Kaelin said with a grin. "In fact, the first present is for you and it's not even under the tree.

"What do you mean?" Molly asked, then her eyes widened as Serogero pushed the bassinet out from behind the tree.

"Mom sent it and we put it together last night," Kaelin explained. "We didn't want to make you try and figure it out after having the baby."

"I never thought," Molly said, tears gathering in her eyes. "I didn't expect..."

"Hey," Kaelin said with a smile. "It's Christmas and this is pretty huge. If we'd told people ahead of time we were celebrating it, we wouldn't have been able to bring all the presents. Have you been following some of the discussions going on?"

Molly shook her head. "I've been focused on other things."

"I know," Kaelin told her. "Aidan has the important stuff saved for you. And he should be here any minute. Trina had some last minute stuff for him."

"Alright," Molly said with a nod. "I just don't know what to do with all of this. With all the other push back we've been getting I never thought there would be actual support."

"Most of the boxes are from mom," Kaelin told her. "Though some of it is from the extra wrapping she sent so anybody who wanted to give gifts could."

"I didn't..." Molly could feel the panic rising in her chest.

"You gave us a daughter," Kaelin said. "That's all that was expected of you."

Molly could feel the tears swimming in her eyes as she looked up at her friend. "Thank you. For everything. I don't know that I could have done all this without you here."

Kaelin smiled. "Of course you could," she said. "You're a pretty tough cookie when you need to be. I'm glad I could be here, though. I wouldn't miss this party for the world."

"Am I late?" Aidan asked, coming through one of the other entrances. "This is probably the earliest I've been up for a holiday in years."

"You're just in time," Kaelin said and straightened. "Let's get you up here with your mom and Mintonar before the baby wakes up. We can do everybody else after."

Aidan wore a suit that mimicked Mintonar's with a more modern Earth cut. It was forest green with Mintonar's family crest worked through it in silver. Trina had added a dark silver waist coat and the combination was stunning. Gone was the slightly awkward teenager she still remembered and in his place stood a man.

"Merry Christmas, mom," he said, leaning down to kiss her cheek.

"Merry Christmas, baby," she told him back.

"I'm not the baby anymore," he told her and reached down to run his finger across his sister's cheek. He'd come to the medical bay the night before after he'd been told it was safe to come and visit and held her while Mintonar ran tests. The awe in his face had made Molly cry though she'd tried her best to hide it when he brought his sister back to her.

"You'll always be my baby," she protested. "But you're right, you're definitely not a baby anymore."

"Ready for pictures?" Kaelin called, raising the camera.

"Yep," Aidan answered. "Where do you want us?"

Kaelin arranged them in front of the Christmas tree with Mindy and Serogero pitching in to move boxes around until she was happy with the pose. Molly in her chair, Mintonar behind her right shoulder and Aidan behind her left, with a glimpse of the baby's face through the blankets. Then she started snapping pictures. They were moved around for different poses and she took several with Aidan holding his sister and looking very much in love with the tiny creature.

She woke up and started fussing and Kaelin declared their time over and moved on to more pictures of everybody else while Molly dealt with the fussy baby. Mintonar moved her away so she could have some privacy to feed the baby and Aidan stepped away to get more cookies for all of them.

Mintonar was called back to the Christmas tree and Molly settled back into the chair, the memory of how to hold a breast-feeding baby coming back with practice. She looked up and glanced down the hall Aidan had come through. Trina and Captain Cretus were standing beneath the mistletoe hung just outside the lounge and kissing.

Molly grinned then looked away from the sweet scene in front of her. It wasn't any of her business but it seemed like they were making progress and that made her happy. They made an appearance in the lounge a few moments later and were drawn into the controlled chaos that was the photo session Kaelin was directing.

When she was done nursing, Molly straightened her dress and cleaned off the baby's face before waving at her family to come and get her for more pictures. The baby was awake and alert and probably would be for a little while longer.

Mintonar came over and stroked a finger down his daughter's cheek and Kaelin snapped a picture. The expression on his face was definitely one worth capturing. He picked her up and Aidan came behind Molly's chair to push her towards the Christmas tree.

Dorcas and Barruch came out of the kitchen carrying more plates of cookies to the cheers of all those assembled and Kaelin took pictures of the additional cookies then pulled Dorcas in for more pictures. Some time during the festivities, Chaegar slipped into the room unnoticed and started piling cookies on a small plate, his mouth turned into a determined frown. He left with the plate of cookies but not before he watched Dorcas join the happy group of people.

Once Dorcas' pictures were completed, Mintonar cleared his throat and everybody went quiet. He nodded to Kaelin and she turned on the camera to record. The announcement was going out across the ship and would then be transmitted to the space station and the planet.

"Greetings," he said. "To the people of Earth and the passengers on the Forward Hope. On this Earth day of celebration, I wish to show you the greatest gift I have ever received. Early this morning, my mate Maw-lee gave birth to my daughter, Lilianha. She is the first human-Orvax baby and, we hope, the first baby born to a time of peace and prosperity between our peoples."

Kaelin moved to get a view of the yawning, contented infant, before ending the transmission.

"To Lili, the first baby of peace!" Mindy said, and raised a glass she'd been handing around.

Aidan handed one to his mother that sparkled but her first tentative sniff of it told her it was sparkling apple juice rather than something alcoholic. He had one as well and raised it to her before they both drank.

"The first," Aidan said. "And let's hope not the last."

"Amen," Molly agreed, and took another sip. "But not from me for a while."

Epilogue

Chaegar made his way to the holding cells with his plate of cookies. He'd made this trip a lot, far more times than he wanted to admit to anybody else, but he had the feeling it was going to be his last one.

The woman sitting in the cell looked up at him when he approached and sighed. She looked disheveled, her hair pulled back from her face but otherwise plain, and it looked like she'd been chewing on her fingernails again.

"Merry Christmas," Chaegar said, holding up the plate of cookies. He hated the hope in his voice and that she knew it was there.

"Molly had the baby," she said. "On Christmas?"

He nodded and she shook her head. "I can't believe she let him touch her like that. That's she'd want him to touch her like that. It just doesn't make sense to me. He's not even human!"

Chaegar sighed and put the cookies on a tray outside the holding cell. "I can't speak for Molly or Mintonar," he told her. "But there are many delights to be had in the arms of the right Orvax."

She shuddered. "Not after what I saw," she said. "Or what I felt. Whatever that was, it certainly wasn't pleasure."

"It's supposed to be," Chaegar told her. "I'd be happy to—"

"I'm sure you would," she said, cutting off the offer.

He'd made the same offer almost every day since they'd gotten on board the ship. The few times he'd been gone over night with the shuttle, he always came back and spent time sitting with her. She looked tired and he didn't blame her.

He sighed and she looked at him. "Jamie, I'm sorry you were brought into this," he said. "You were just doing your job and I hoped you would come around. I hate seeing you in here, but I can't get you out unless you're willing to promise to behave. And I'd have to be able to vouch not only for your good behavior but your intent to join the mission."

"And the only way to do all of that is to agree to sleep with you?" she sneered. He could tell her heart wasn't in it, but it wasn't with him, either.

"Not the only way," he said. "But the easiest. I'm not going to ask you to accept me as your mate, I think it might be too late for that anyway, but please consider it."

She looked away and he took another deep breath.

"Alright," he said. "I understand your people give gifts at Christmas. There's not much I can give you that you would accept so I'll give you the one thing you've asked for that I can give you."

"You're going to let me out?" she asked, her head snapped around to look at him.

He shook his head. "I can't. That's not my decision to make. But I'm going to leave you alone and stop asking you to join me. You don't enjoy my company and I'm just making us both miserable by pursuing this so I'm going to stop."

She stared at him for a long moment. "I'm sorry," she said.

"I am, too," he said softly. "Enjoy the cookies."

He turned and walked away.

"Merry Christmas," she called after him.

It hurt to hear, and he closed his eyes briefly once he was out of sight. Whatever hope he'd had for having his own mate had crumbled slowly over the last few weeks.

Author's Note

Hello Lovers!

Thank you so much for reading The Alien's Christmas Baby! I hope you enjoyed this brief interlude in the life of our favorite couples. They have so much coming in the new year, it's nice to take a moment and let them rest and welcome a new life into the world.

What's next? Well, coming up is *Captivating the Alien Captain* where we get to see what happens after that kiss under the mistletoe. Will Trina take the love she's being offered? Can Captain Cretus convince her he can enhance her happiness? You'll have to read the next book to find out!

I don't know about you but I started listening to Christmas music early this year and not just because it helped put me in the mood for a party on a certain space ship. When I was trying to write the teaser/description for this story, it kept trying to come out as a Christmas carol. At the insistence of my writing group, I've included it for your enjoyment.

(To the tune of Christmas is Coming)
Christmas is coming, Molly's getting fat
Please to eat a cookie in the shape of a hat
If you haven't got a santa hat a Christmas tree will do
If you haven't got a Christmas tree than God Bless You!

Christmas is coming, Mindy's getting fat?

Please to make a baby with your own Orvax

If you can't make a baby, a Christmas dress will do

If you can't make a Christmas dress then a baby-sitter will do!

As always, if you enjoyed the story, leave me a review and let me know! If you want to be among the first to hear when the next book is out or get occasional glimpses of my usually boring though occasionally exciting life, you can check my website cvwalterauthor.com or follow the newsletter at cvwalter.substack.com

Until next time,

Love,

C.V.

About the Author

C.V. Walter, author of Mates by Design, is currently working on her alien romance series. She thinks the family that you choose is more important than the ones you were born into. She lives in Colorado with her two husbands, two kids and a variable number of pets. To hear more about upcoming releases, sign up for the mailing list at cvwalterauthor.com

Other Works

Alien Brides

The Alien's Accidental Bride
Bound to the Alien Engineer
Wed to the Alien Prince
Country Roads
The Alien's Christmas Baby
Captivating the Alien Captain
Pursued by the Alien Pilot

Blessed Curse

Mates by Design
Hunting Red
The Bear and the Bees

Myths of Lust and Love

Marble Goddess
Gift of the Gods
Invisible Lover

Evil Sorceress in Training

In The Dungeon
In The Tower
In The Circle
On The Rack
Sacrifice